One Starry Night

The wild animals featured in this book could all be found in the
Holy Land at the time of the traditional nativity story. They are the
untamed cousins of the domesticated animals named in the text.

sheep—mountain sheep   goat—ibex   cat—cheetah   donkey—wild ass
cow—wild ox   pig—wild boar   dog—jackal   dove—rock dove

MARGARET K. McELDERRY BOOKS • An imprint of Simon & Schuster Children's Publishing Division • 1230
Avenue of the Americas, New York, New York 10020 • Text copyright © 2011 by Lauren Thompson • Illustrations
copyright © 2011 by Jonathan Bean • All rights reserved, including the right of reproduction in whole or in part in any
form. • MARGARET K. McELDERRY BOOKS is a trademark of Simon & Schuster, Inc. • For information about special
discounts for bulk purchases, please contact Simon & Schuster Special Sales at 1-866-506-1949 or business
@simonandschuster.com. • The Simon & Schuster Speakers Bureau can bring authors to your live event. For more
information or to book an event, contact the Simon & Schuster Speakers Bureau at 1-866-248-3049 or visit our
website at www.simonspeakers.com. • The text for this book is set in Bernhard Modern. • The illustrations for this book
are rendered in pencil and colored digitally. • Manufactured in China • 0711 SCP • 10 9 8 7 6 5 4 3 2 1 •
CIP data for this book is available from the Library of Congress. • ISBN 978-0-689-82851-5

FIRST
EDITION

One Starry Night

by Lauren Thompson *illustrated by* Jonathan Bean

Margaret K. McElderry Books
New York   London   Toronto   Sydney

To Owen, and every doveling everywhere—L. T.

To my nephews, Stephen and Izayah—J. B.

One starry night

a sheep watched over her lamb

I am here

a cow watched over her calf

always near

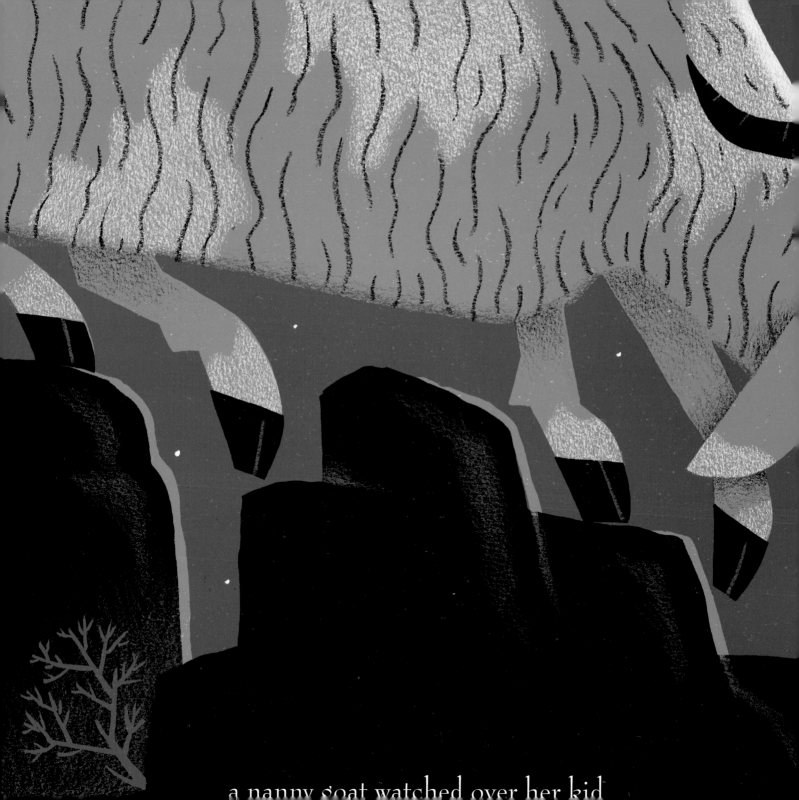

a nanny goat watched over her kid

never far

a pig watched over her piglet

wherever you are

a cat watched over her kitten

caring for you

a dog watched over her pup

whatever you do

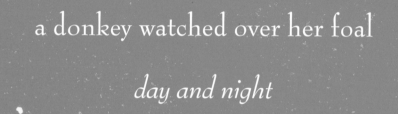

a donkey watched over her foal

day and night

and a dove watched over her doveling

my love is bright

On this starry night

Mary and Joseph watched over
their newborn babe

beloved one

and the world was filled with love

God's will be done

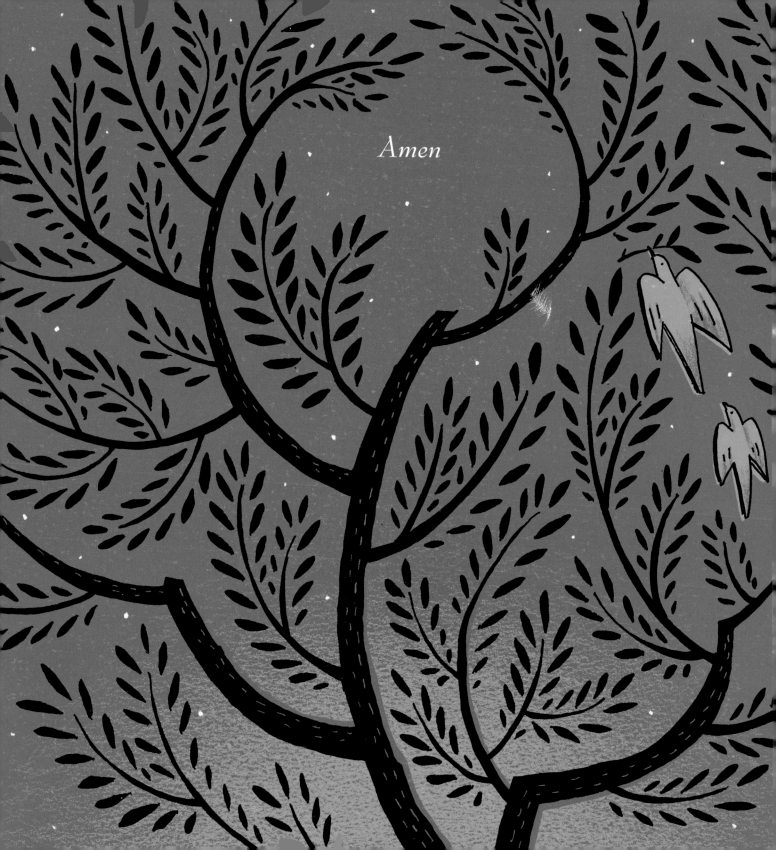

Amen